For the
children
at the
Arthur F.
Turner
Branch
Yolo County
Library

Ed Young
1985

UP A TREE

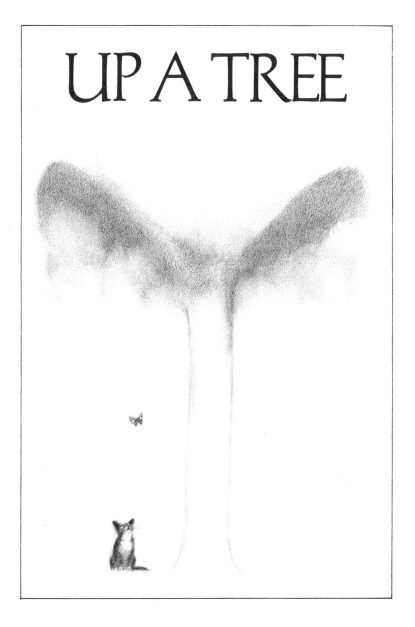

UP A TREE

ED YOUNG

E
c. 2

Harper & Row, Publishers

To Siao Mao, O.D., Shimi, and Eeni,
who vastly enriched me
with their world and ways

Up a Tree
Copyright © 1983 by Ed Young
All rights reserved. No part of this book may be
used or reproduced in any manner whatsoever without
written permission except in the case of brief quotations
embodied in critical articles and reviews. Printed in
the Unted States of America. For information address
Harper & Row, Publishers, Inc., 10 East 53rd Street,
New York, N.Y. 10022. Published simultaneously in
Canada by Fitzhenry & Whiteside Limited, Toronto.
First Edition
Library of Congress Cataloging in Publication Data
Young, Ed.
   Up a tree.

   Summary: A cat finds himself up a tree and won't come
down until supper passes him by.
   [1. Cats—Fiction.   2. Stories without words]
I. Title.
PZ7.Y855Up 1983   [E]   82-47733
ISBN 0-06-026813-1
ISBN 0-06-026814-X (lib. bdg.)

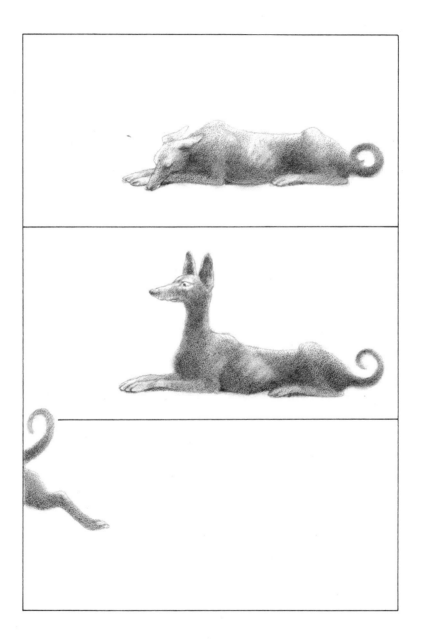

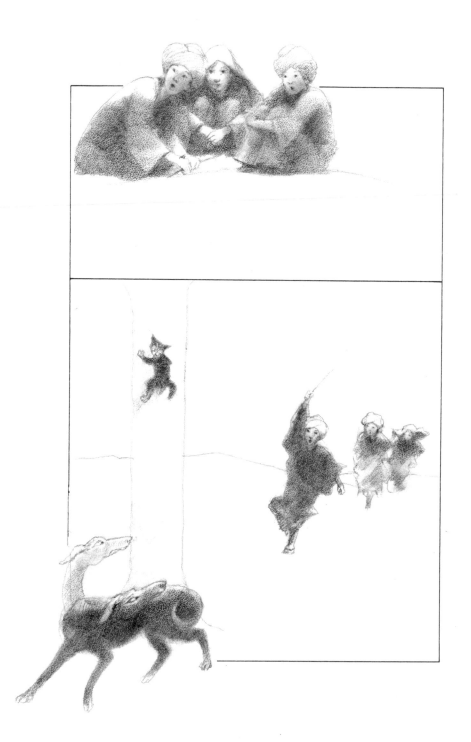

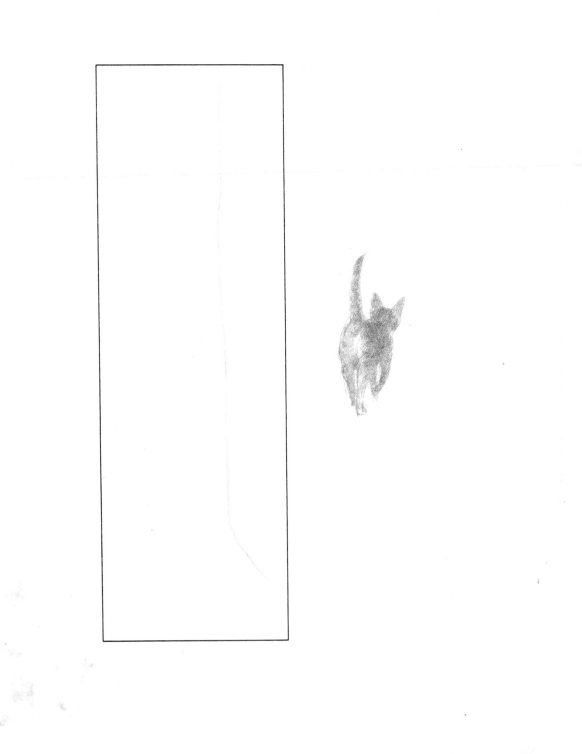